For Hope

It was already Tuesday, and Toot's birthday was on Friday. Puddle wanted to get him the best present ever.

Toot and Puddle
A Present for Toot

by Holly Hobbie

A division of Hodder Headline Limited

First published in the US in 1998 by
Little, Brown & Company

First published in Canada in 1998 by
Little, Brown & Company (Canada) Limited

First published in Britain in 2000 by
Hodder Children's Books
a division of Hodder Headline Limited
338 Euston Road
London NW1 3BH

ISBN: 0 7500 3021 6 (HB)
ISBN: 0 7500 3022 4 (PB)

10 9 8 7 6 5 4 3 2 1

British Library Cataloguing in Publication Data
A catalogue record for this book is available from the British Library.

Printed in Hong Kong

The paintings for this book were done in watercolour. The text type was set in Optima, and the display type was set in Windsor Light and Poetica.

"What do you want for your birthday?" Puddle asked.
"I don't need a thing," said Toot, who was busy birdwatching.
"Just tell me," Puddle pleaded.
"Surprise me," Toot said. He pointed. "A nuthatch!"
"Toot," Puddle said, "I'm serious."
"OK," Toot said. "Anything."

Going shopping made Puddle nervous.

In the Good Read Bookshop, he saw many books he'd like, but he couldn't find the right book for Toot.

In Hardy's Hardware, Puddle fell in love with a red-handled hammer . . .

In Ted's Sport Shop, his favourite thing was a big shiny bowling ball, but Toot had never liked bowling.

And he wanted everything in Kate's Kitchen Shop. But it's not Puddle's birthday, he reminded himself. It's Toot's birthday.

Puddle returned home empty-handed – and very tired.

The next day Puddle slipped off to town again while Toot was having breakfast. He spent all morning traipsing through shops. Toot is special, he thought – that's the problem.

Puddle liked everything he saw in Pip's Pet Shop.

But Toot had travelled all over the world, Puddle thought.
He had seen *amazing* animals.
"Toot is too special for ordinary pets," he said aloud.

“Maybe,” a strange voice said.
“Excuse me?” Puddle said.
“Excuse me,” the voice said back.
“Hello?” Puddle said, looking around.
“Hello,” repeated the voice.
“Are you talking to me?” Puddle asked.

THE CAT
THE DOG
Your 1ST

Puddle couldn't stop thinking about Tulip. He had just enough money to buy an expensive pet. But was Tulip the right present? Then Puddle remembered the words Tulip had spoken: "I need a place to live."

On Thursday Toot and Puddle had a picnic.
"Your birthday is almost here," Puddle said. "Isn't there one thing you want?"
"I thought you were going to surprise me," said Toot.
"Maybe I will."

Puddle was afraid he had made a terrible mistake. His friend didn't want parrots around here. And if Tulip was unhappy at Woodcock Pocket, it would be Puddle's fault.

Poor Tulip, he thought.

"Tulip, where are you?" he called softly. His heart was pounding.
"I'm freezing," said the parrot. She stuck her head out from under an old blanket. "You didn't tell me it would be so cold."

"Only for tonight," Puddle said. "It's warm in the house."
"It's pretty lonely, too," Tulip said. "Compared to Pip's Pet Shop."
"It's not at all lonely in the house," Puddle said. "But I'll keep you company out here tonight."

"Are you awake?" Puddle asked.
"Totally," Tulip said.
"I was thinking," said Puddle. "You don't have to stay at Woodcock Pocket if you don't want to."
Tulip didn't say anything.
"I mean," Puddle went on, "there are other places to live."
"I know *that,*" Tulip said. She added, "I think I'll stay."

Friday came.
"You can't go in the shed," Puddle told Toot.
"All right," Toot said. He had a big smile on his pink face.

It's time to party, Puddle thought.

"Puddle, what in the world do you have on your head?" Toot asked.

"Something special," Puddle said nervously.

"Surprise," Puddle said.
"Surprise," Tulip said.
"Who are you?" Toot asked.
"Well, it looks like I'm your present," said Tulip.

"And now," Tulip said, "*I* have a little something for Toot."
She reached around with her beak and plucked out one bright red tail feather. "Happy birthday!" she said.
Toot stared. "It's beautiful," he said. "Thank you." And he stuck it in his favourite hat right away.
Puddle was just as surprised as Toot. "Didn't that hurt?" he asked.
"It just pinched," said Tulip.

"Well, I guess that wasn't an ordinary birthday with ordinary presents," Puddle said. "Was it?"
"It was extraordinary," Toot said.
"You could say *exotic,*" said Tulip.